Rosy Noses, Freezing Toes

YOUNG YEARLING BOOKS YOU WILL ENJOY:

The Pee Wee Scout Books by Judy Delton

COOKIES AND CRUTCHES
CAMP GHOST-AWAY
LUCKY DOG DAYS
BLUE SKIES, FRENCH FRIES
GRUMPY PUMPKINS
PEANUT-BUTTER PILGRIMS
A PEE WEE CHRISTMAS
THAT MUSHY STUFF
SPRING SPROUTS
THE POOPED TROOP
THE PEE WEE JUBILEE
BAD, BAD BUNNIES
ROSY NOSES, FREEZING TOES

YEARLING BOOKS/YOUNG YEARLINGS/YEARLING CLASSICS are designed especially to entertain and enlighten young people. Patricia Reilly Giff, consultant to this series, received the bachelor's degree from Marymount College. She holds the master's degree in history from St. John's University, and a Professional Diploma in Reading from Hofstra University. She was a teacher and reading consultant for many years, and is the author of numerous books for young readers.

Rosy Noses, Freezing Toes

JUDY DELTON

Illustrated by Alan Tiegreen

A YOUNG YEARLING BOOK

Published by
Dell Publishing
a division of
Bantam Doubleday Dell Publishing Group, Inc.
666 Fifth Avenue
New York, New York 10103

ISBN: 0-440-40384-7

Printed in the United States of America

November 1990

10 9 8 7 6 5 4 3 2 1

CWO

For Shirley and Herbert Gould, and for
Mrs. Finley, Ruth, and Carol, with warm
Boston and New Hampshire memories

With thanks to Ingrid van der Leeden

Contents

CHAPTER 1

Who Stole the Vase?

"Mrs. Peters," called Lisa Ronning, "Tim Noon hasn't got a good deed to report."

"He never has a good deed," said Roger White.

"Have too," said Tim.

"Have not," said Roger.

"Have too," said Tim.

"Mrs. Peters, Tim kicked me!" cried Roger.

Mrs. Peters held up her hand. She gave the boys what Molly Duff called a teacher-

look. But Mrs. Peters was not a teache was a Scout leader. She was the leader of eleven Pee Wee Scouts in Troop 23. Every Tuesday they all met in her basement around a big round table. They helped people and earned badges. They had lots of fun together.

"Roger's right," whispered Molly to her friend Mary Beth Kelly. "Tim never does any good deeds."

"Scouts are kind to each other," said Mrs. Peters. "Tim's good deeds are his own business."

Tim stuck his tongue out at Roger.

"I have an announcement to make," Mrs. Peters went on.

The Pee Wees sat up at attention. Sometimes announcements meant parties, or picnics. Announcements could be fun.

"It can't be a picnic," said Tracy Barnes. "There's too much snow outside."

Molly and Mary Beth laughed when they

oasting hot dogs in the snow.
s and parkas on.
chup would freeze," shouted

"Our soda pop would turn to icicles!" hooted Patty Baker.

"Do we have to sell something?" asked Sonny Betz. "Like donuts?" Sonny's mother was assistant Scout leader.

Mrs. Peters shook her head.

"We're not selling donuts." She laughed. "This is a different kind of announcement."

"Maybe she is going to have another baby!" whispered Rachel Meyers.

Mrs. Peters had one baby. His name was Nick. He took his nap during the meeting.

"Do you remember the little Chinese vase I put your flowers in last summer?"

This wasn't the kind of announcement they were waiting to hear, thought Molly.

Rachel was waving her hand. "Do you

mean the one you put my rose in, Mrs. Peters?"

Their leader nodded.

"You said my rose was so pretty, you would get out your special antique vase to put it in," said Rachel proudly.

Kevin Moe waved his hand. "I remember that vase," he said. "You said it was valuable because it was an antique."

Mrs. Peters nodded again. Kevin liked valuable things. He wanted to be a rich businessman and earn lots of money. He even wanted to be mayor of their city someday.

"That vase seems to have disappeared," said Mrs. Peters. "I can't find it anywhere. It's a mystery where it could have got to."

The Pee Wees loved mysteries.

"It is very valuable," Mrs. Peters went on. "It is imported from China. And on top of that, it is an antique that has been in the family for years."

Did Mrs. Peters think that one of the Pee Wee Scouts had stolen it? thought Molly.

"I didn't take it!" shouted Tim.

"Me neither," said Sonny. "What's an antique?"

"An antique is something very old," said Mrs. Peters.

"My mom throws out old stuff," said Tim.

"You don't throw out antiques," said Rachel. "My mother collects them. She has a china plate over one hundred years old."

"Who wants to eat on some old dish?" asked Tim. "It's probably all dirty and full of cracks."

"It is not!" said Rachel with her hands on her hips. "We don't eat on dirty dishes."

Mrs. Peters had to hold up her hand again. "I just thought maybe my Scouts could scout it out," she said.

"We'll find it," said Kevin.

"Where was it last?" asked Roger, like a detective.

"Is there a reward?" asked Sonny.

Mrs. Peters laughed.

"There will certainly be a reward to whoever finds it."

The Scouts looked under furniture. They looked over furniture. They looked in the garage and they looked in Mrs. Peters's laundry tubs.

"It wouldn't be in a laundry tub!" said Rachel.

"It must be somewhere," said Mrs. Peters. "It couldn't have walked away by itself."

The Scouts looked and looked. Finally they had to give up. "I'll just have to call the insurance company and report it," said Mrs. Peters. Their leader explained to the Pee Wees that when you owned something valuable, you insured it. "Then the insurance company pays you for it if you lose it," she added.

The rest of the meeting the Pee Wees told about good deeds they had done. They talked

about Christmas coming soon. They cut out paper snowmen with arms and legs that moved. Then they said their Pee Wee Scout pledge and sang their Pee Wee Scout song.

On the way home from the meeting, Kenny Baker, who was Patty's twin brother, said, "I think somebody stole that vase of Mrs. Peters's. I'll bet one of the Pee Wee Scouts took it."

CHAPTER 2
Fiddle and Drum Talk

The Pee Wee Scouts were eager for Christmas vacation to begin. They counted the days of school left. They were all in second grade.

The next Tuesday at the Scout meeting, Kenny said, "Did you find the thief yet, Mrs. Peters?"

"What thief, Kenny?" she asked.

"The one who stole your vase. I can find him for you," he said.

"No one stole the vase, Kenny. It's lost. I called the insurance company and they are going to send me a check."

"I don't like it," said Kenny. "That vase couldn't have got up and walked away by itself."

"Well, we'll just put it out of our minds now and get on with our holiday plans," said Mrs. Peters.

"The next badge we earn," she went on, "has something to do with the holidays." Then she held up a brand-new badge the Pee Wees had never seen.

The badge was white, and it had a big black musical note on it, with a little black flag on its stem.

"Ohhh," said the Scouts. "It's pretty!"

All the badges were pretty. Molly loved badges. She couldn't wait to get the next one.

"This is the music badge," Mrs. Peters went on. "You can earn this badge by singing or playing a short piece on any musical instrument. You may even just tell about the life of someone who wrote songs."

"I play the piano," said Rachel. "Would it

be all right if I played a song, *and* told about the life of a composer?"

"Yes, of course, Rachel," said Mrs. Peters. "I thought that since the holidays are so close, we would have our little musical program the Saturday before Christmas."

"I can't play anything," said Tim.

"I can't either," said Sonny.

"Then you may either sing, or tell us about someone musical," said the leader.

"Because it is almost Christmas, I think the song you choose should be a holiday song, like 'Jingle Bells,' or maybe a Hanukkah song," said Mrs. Peters.

"I'd like to have the program right here at our house," she added. "But we don't have a piano."

"We could have it at my house," volunteered Rachel. "We have a big music room."

"That is very nice of you, Rachel," said their leader. "But I'd like to have a piano here anyway, so that we can all sing together at our meetings. It would be nice to have music to accompany our Scout song, and we could learn new songs together. Songs for all the holidays."

The Pee Wees cheered. A piano would be fun. Singing was fun. But how would Mrs. Peters get enough money to buy one? wondered Molly.

"I'm going to sleep on it," Mrs. Peters said mysteriously.

Mrs. Peters and the Pee Wees planned the music show.

"I'm wearing my recital outfit," said Rachel. "It's got sequins on it."

"I'm not wearing anything," said Sonny, "because I'm not coming. I can't play anything."

"Your mother will help you decide what to do," said Mrs. Peters. "Now let's have some chocolate cupcakes I baked this morning."

Mrs. Peters passed out the cupcakes to

everyone. She got baby Nick up from his nap and he had one too.

"How about Lucky, and Tiny?" said Kenny. "They feel left out."

Tiny was Mrs. Peters's dog. Lucky was Troop 23's mascot.

"Cake isn't good for dogs," said Mrs. Peters. "I'll give them a doggie treat."

"Arf!" said the dogs when they saw the box.

"What are you going to do for the show?" Molly asked Mary Beth as they ate their cupcakes.

"I don't know," she answered.

"Why don't we sing?" said Lisa. "The three of us can sing together. I like 'Silent Night.' "

Molly looked doubtful. She liked to sing. But she thought she didn't sing very well. Not well enough for a real show.

"I'm going to play 'White Christmas' on my drums," said Roger.

The girls snickered. "How can you play a song on your drums?" asked Mary Beth. "Bong bong bong."

"A drum can't play a song," said Lisa.

Roger looked shocked. "What do you think those guys in bands are doing?" he said. "They play songs."

Molly looked doubtful. "I don't think they play alone," she said.

"Well, I'm better than those guys," said Roger. "I can play 'White Christmas' all alone."

The Pee Wees helped clean up the room. Then they sang their Scout song together. Molly thought about how nice it would sound with a piano.

On the way home, everyone talked about what they would play or what they would sing or what they would do.

"Almost everyone is telling about a composer," said Tracy. "I don't think there will be much music."

"I'm not coming," said Sonny again.

"You have to come, or you won't get your badge," said Molly.

Sonny looked upset. But the next morning on the playground he looked even more upset. He pushed one of the first-graders on the slide, and made her cry.

"What's the matter with you?" said Molly. The last time Sonny had been so mean was when he didn't like his mom's new boyfriend, Larry.

Sonny kicked the slide. "My mom is making me take violin lessons."

"You can't learn to play the violin in time for the show, can you?" asked Molly.

Sonny blew his nose. "She always wanted me to take violin. She says now is as good a time as any. The teacher told her by the time of the show I'd be able to play the first line of 'Jingle Bells.' "

Molly tried to picture Sonny with a violin.

"You're lucky," said Molly. "You'll be the only one who plays a violin."

Sonny looked a little brighter. "Really?" he said.

"No other kids get to take violin lessons."

Molly added *get to* because without it it sounded like only weird kids took violin.

Sonny began to smile again. He smiled until he told the other Scouts about his lessons.

"Hey, Maestro, where's your long beard?" shouted Roger.

"The violin?" yelled Kevin. "There's no money in the violin. You should take guitar lessons and go on TV."

Some of the Pee Wees ran around plucking imaginary strings.

Sonny went into a funk all over again. But the next day his mom picked him up after school to take him to his violin lesson. In the car was a big black case. And in the case was Sonny's violin.

"It's as big as Sonny!" shouted Roger. "We could put Sonny in that violin case!"

Poor Sonny, thought Molly. Somehow he always ends up being picked on. And this time Molly didn't see how she could help.

CHAPTER 3

Christmas Shopping and Sledding

Time was going by fast. Every day the girls practiced their song for the music show. They had decided to sing "Rudolph the Red-Nosed Reindeer." They planned to paint their noses red for the show.

At practice Molly thought Mary Beth sang too high.

Molly thought Lisa sang too low.

Molly thought that she herself sang just right.

"I can't wait to get that badge!" said Mary Beth.

"I wonder if Sonny and Roger will get their badges," said Molly.

"Sonny has lessons three times a week now," laughed Lisa. "But the violin is hard to learn. My dad said so."

One day the Pee Wee Scouts went Christmas shopping together at the mall. Molly got her mother a new hairbrush. She got her dad a new tie with red and green stripes. She got her grandma some bubble bath. And Mary Beth a book. Mary Beth loved to read. Then all of her saved-up allowance was gone.

"Rachel has twenty dollars to spend on Hanukkah presents," said Tracy. "I heard her say so."

"How could she get that much money?" asked Patty. "No allowance is that big."

"Her dad is a dentist," said Molly. "Dentists make lots and lots of money. Just putting fillings in your teeth."

"How could those little tiny fillings get him lots of money?" said Tracy.

"I don't have any fillings because I don't eat any candy," said Sonny.

"I saw you eat candy," said Roger.

The Pee Wees watched Rachel shop. She was still buying presents after the others had spent all their money.

"I got my mom this genuine silver candle snuffer," said Rachel, holding up something that looked to Molly like a long spoon upside down. "You put it over the candle and it goes out, 'poof,' just like that."

"Why can't she blow out candles like everybody else?" demanded Roger.

Rachel sighed and rolled her eyes at Roger.

"She won't get her wish if she doesn't blow," said Tim.

"These aren't birthday candles, silly," said Rachel.

Some of the Pee Wees got baby Nick something too. And some of them even bought Lucky and Tiny a holiday treat.

"My mom is getting Mrs. Peters a present," said Rachel. "It's a silk scarf."

Most of the Scouts were making Mrs. Peters a gift.

"She said she likes things we make ourselves better," said Lisa.

"Everybody says that," scoffed Rachel. "But nobody really means it. Nobody likes homemade gifts."

Rachel may be right, thought Molly. Her mother always said it was the thought that counted, but who wanted a lopsided potholder anyway? Who wanted any potholder, come to think of it.

"I'm going to be real rich someday," said Kevin. "Then I'm not going to make any of my presents. I'm going to buy everything in the store. I might even buy the store!"

When everyone had spent all their money, the Scouts took their gifts home and wrapped them. Then they got out sleds and toboggans and plastic saucers and dragged them to the park. They climbed the highest hill in town and slid down the icy path made for sliding.

"This thing is too small," said Sonny, kicking his little sled that had rusty runners. "It sticks in the snow."

"It's a baby sled," said Kenny. "Only baby sleds have sides on them."

"Hey, Sonny, go home and get that violin case! You can slide down real fast in that!" said Roger.

The Pee Wees broke into laughter. Except Molly. She felt sorry for Sonny. Everyone always laughed at him.

"He's such a baby," said Tracy. "No wonder people laugh."

"It's not his fault," said Molly. "It's his mother's. She always makes him do things no one else does."

Maybe she should talk to Mrs. Betz about Sonny. Maybe Mrs. Betz didn't know that other kids didn't take violin lessons or ride bikes with training wheels when they were seven. Once she had heard her own mother say, "That Sonny Betz is going to be a handful by the time he gets to high school."

Molly couldn't imagine Sonny in high school. When she tried, all she could see was someone taller with a baby face and a whine.

"I wonder what Sonny will be like in high school," said Molly to Mary Beth and Lisa.

"He'll be driving a car with training wheels!" roared Lisa.

When it got dark, the Pee Wees started home. Sonny sat on his sled and wouldn't move. The Scouts took turns pulling him home.

That night Molly and her mother and dad went to get a Christmas tree at the corner lot. The snow was falling and the man who sold the trees had Christmas music on a tape in his warming house.

"That's to get people in the holiday spirit so they buy a tree," said Mr. Duff.

He did buy a tree. It was a wonderful tall tree that touched the ceiling when he set it up at home in the living room. The next afternoon the family decorated it, and Molly's mother and grandma baked cookies in the shape of bells and deer and stars and candles. Molly sprinkled red sugar on them. And she got to lick the cookie bowl.

"Tuesday is the last Pee Wee Scout meeting before Christmas," said Mrs. Duff that evening.

"We have the music show," said Molly. "That will be like a meeting too."

"I think it will be more like a party," laughed Mrs. Duff. "A holiday party."

Molly's mother and dad would be at the party. So would all the other mothers and dads.

Would Mrs. Peters have a piano by then? Would Sonny be able to play the violin by Saturday? And how was Roger going to play a tune with just a drum? Molly wanted all of the Pee Wees to get the music badge. She didn't want them to be laughed at.

When Molly finally fell asleep that night, she dreamed that a policeman came to one of their Scout meetings and took one of the Scouts away for stealing Mrs. Peters's valuable vase. He put the Scout in jail. But Molly didn't know which Scout it was. She couldn't see the face in the dream.

CHAPTER 4

Stage Fright

"Just look," said Mrs. Peters proudly, at the meeting on Tuesday. She was pointing to a piano in her living room.

"It's an old one," she said. "But it sounds wonderful. And every note works!"

Mrs. Peters sat down and played "The First Noel." Everyone clapped.

The piano sounds better than it looks, thought Molly. There were chips in the wood, and lots of scratches.

"I'm going to refinish it next summer," said Mrs. Peters. "Perhaps we will all do it together and get a badge for furniture restoring!"

"Did it cost a lot of money?" Kevin wanted to know.

"It cost exactly the same as the check from the insurance company," said Mrs. Peters. "That old vase paid for this old piano!"

"I'm going to find that vase," said Kevin. "I know it has to be somewhere around here."

"Don't do that now, Kevin," laughed their leader. "If we found it we'd have to give the money back to the insurance company. And to give the money back we'd have to sell our piano!"

"I dreamed that someone stole the vase," said Molly. She didn't add that it was one of the Pee Wees. "If someone stole it we won't ever get it back, so we can keep the piano."

"Unless their conscience bothers them and they return it," said Patty. "Crooks might feel guilty and bring it back so they can sleep better."

"Well, let's hope the vase stays wherever it is, so we can enjoy our piano," laughed Mrs. Peters, playing the Pee Wee Scout song.

Molly had to agree with Mrs. Peters that a piano was a good thing for the Pee Wee Scouts to have.

They sang Scout songs and Christmas songs and Hanukkah songs.

Mrs. Peters even played a march and they marched up and down the basement stairs and through the living room and dining room.

"It's easier to sing when there's piano music," said Lisa.

"That's because you can't hear all the mistakes you make," said Rachel. "But you have to sing alone at the show."

She was right. They couldn't depend on

background music at the music show. Mrs. Peters said each Scout or group of Scouts had to do it themselves.

"We don't need any old piano to sing," said Lisa.

Christmas got closer and closer. And the music show got closer and closer. The houses on Molly's block had trees up and lights in the windows and wreaths on the front doors. People carried bright packages with red bows on them. The snow sparkled in the sun and under evening streetlights. The Pee Wees were getting excited.

At last it was Saturday. The last Saturday before Christmas. The day of the music show.

When the Scouts got to Mrs. Peters's house they were surprised. Instead of the furniture in her living room, folding chairs were set up in rows. And in the dining room, on the table, was a wonderful Christmas tree with the lights on, even though it was daytime.

"There was no room for a tree on the floor," laughed Mr. Peters, who was home for the weekend show.

"Come in, come in!" Mrs. Peters was saying to the guests at the door.

Mothers and fathers and Scouts poured into the house. They put their coats in Nick's bedroom, and took some green punch from the dining-room table.

"I made it myself," said Mr. Peters, who was holding Nick. "It has ginger ale in it to make it fizz."

The Pee Wees liked drinks that fizzed.

"The bubbles go up your nose," said Tim, making a face.

All of a sudden there was a commotion at the door. There was a bang and a thump and a thud.

"Here is our drummer!" said Mrs. Peters, clearing a space for Roger to come in.

"Why does he need so *many*?" asked Rachel. "I only need one piano. How can he play all those at one time?"

Molly wondered that herself as Roger lugged in drum after drum.

"A drummer plays drums, not a drum," said Kevin.

When Roger got in and settled and Mr. Peters found a place for the drums, there was another noise at the door. Lucky and Tiny began to bark. This was a lot of excitement for them.

Mr. Peters opened the door and the Pee Wees saw something big and black.

"It's a monster!" yelled Tim.

"It's a violin case!" shouted Kevin.

"It looks like it's walking in alone," laughed Kenny.

"Come in!" said Mr. Peters to Sonny. Behind Sonny were Mrs. Betz and Larry. They were walking arm in arm.

"They're in love," whispered Rachel.

Molly knew that. Mrs. Betz was in love with the fire chief. She had met him when the Pee Wee Scouts had gone to the fire station for a tour.

"Here is the violin virtuoso," said Larry, patting Sonny on the top of his head.

"What does that mean?" asked Roger. "It sounds like some kind of spaghetti."

"I think it means something like genius," said Kevin. "We'll soon see what kind of a genius Sonny is."

The living room was filling up, thought Molly. "It's good we only had to bring our voices," she said.

"Yeah, they don't take up any room, anyway," said Mary Beth.

Mrs. Peters was counting noses. "I think we are all here!" she said. Then she said, "I want to welcome all of you today to our little holiday music fest."

She held up the music badges with the little notes on them. Oohs and aahs filled the room.

The Pee Wee Scouts were nervous.

"I wish we were first," said Molly. "I have butterflies in my stomach."

"I never get stage fright," said Rachel. "My mom says I'm a born professional."

But Molly wasn't first. Kenny was first. No one knew what he was going to do when he got up. He had no instrument. He didn't sing. And he didn't tell about a composer. What he did was whistle.

"Whistling isn't music!" shouted Roger. Mrs. Peters put her finger on her lips for Roger to hush up.

"It is too," said Kevin. "I saw a professional whistler on TV."

"I saw him too," said Tim. "He got this guy in the black shorts down on the mat and sat on him."

"That's wrestler, dummy," said Kevin. "I saw a whistler, not a wrestler."

Now Mrs. Peters was frowning. And Kenny was whistling "Frosty the Snow Man."

It really sounds like "Frosty the Snow Man," thought Molly. Kenny knew the whole song. He whistled it twice. Molly felt like singing along.

When he finished, everyone clapped long and hard.

"That's very good, Kenny," said Mrs. Peters. "I had no idea you could whistle so well."

After that some of the Scouts told about composers.

". . . and that's how Irwin Berlin wrote the song 'White Christmas,' " concluded Tim.

"Irving," said Mrs. Peters. "Not Irwin. His name was Irving Berlin."

Molly was getting impatient. And she was worried about Roger and Sonny. And then, when she wasn't expecting it, Mrs. Peters called her name.

"We have a little singing trio next," she said.

It was time. Molly was ready.

CHAPTER 5
Howling and Screeching

Molly and the girls began to sing "Rudolph the Red-Nosed Reindeer." Their voices sounded weak and lonely, Molly thought. Her knees felt weak too, and her stomach still ached. This must be stage fright, said Molly to herself.

Mary Beth forgot the words to the second verse. Then Lisa got nervous and forgot them too. All of a sudden Molly was singing all alone. Molly tried to sing loud enough for the three of them. She began to enjoy being the star! She was sorry when she

came to the chorus and the other two joined her!

"Let's do it again," she whispered to the others.

This time none of them had stage fright. No one sang too high. No one sang too low. And no one forgot the words.

"What a nice solo that was by Molly," said Mrs. Betz when the girls sat down.

"What solo?" said Lisa. "You didn't have a solo."

"When you forgot the second verse," said Molly. "They thought it was a solo."

No one had noticed the mistake. They sang well enough to get their badge!

The next person to perform was Rachel. Rachel had on her recital dress. Rachel sparkled. She walked to the piano and curtsied. Her gold bracelet and ring sparkled in the light too. She looked like she was on the stage every day. She surely did not have stage fright.

"I am going to play a medley," she announced. "A medley of Hanukkah songs."

Then she sat down on Mrs. Peters's new piano stool and ran her hands up and down the keyboard like pianists Molly had seen on the public television station. It sounded beautiful. And she hadn't even begun the songs yet!

"That's just like Rachel," grumbled Roger. "Using all my time up. She can't play one song, no, she has to play a whole bunch of them!"

Rachel did play a bunch of songs. She added lots of frills and flourishes, Molly noticed. When she finished, the crowd clapped loud. Louder than they had for Molly and Mary Beth and Lisa. Rachel bowed and for a minute Molly thought she was going to sit down at the piano and start all over again. Someone was yelling, "Encore! Encore!"

"That means play some more," said Kevin. "It's her dad yelling that!"

Rachel finally left the piano, and it was Roger's turn.

"Only Sonny's left, after him," whispered Kenny.

Mr. Peters helped Roger line all of his drums up in front of him. Roger had a big smile on his face. He raised his drumsticks and began to play.

Bang bang bang. Bang boom bang. Boom boom boom. Boom boom bang.

"You can sing along if you want to," called Roger.

Everyone smiled politely. But no one sang.

Roger hit one drum and then another. He went up and down the line of drums, hitting them all.

"They all sound alike," whispered Mary Beth to Molly.

"What's he playing?" asked Kevin.

Mrs. Peters was frowning.

She's probably wondering how she can give Roger a music badge, thought Molly. Was this music? It didn't sound like music to Molly.

"Now the second verse," said Roger. Bang bang bang. Boom bang boom. Boom boom boom.

Roger played and played. It looked like hard work, banging the drums so hard. When he'd finished, Roger was sweating. He bowed and everyone clapped politely.

Rachel was waving her hand. "That wasn't a song," she said.

"It was 'White Christmas,' " said Roger. "I played 'White Christmas.' All the verses."

"It didn't sound like it," said Lisa. "It didn't go up and down like a song does."

"It didn't even have a tune," said Tracy crossly. "That's not fair."

Mrs. Peters walked to the front of the room. She held her hand up to stop the Scouts from complaining.

"Not all music is alike," she said. "Some music has a tune and some doesn't. Some you can sing to, and some you can't. Drums are one kind of music, and they are hard to play."

"See?" said Roger. "I told you."

"Ha," said Kevin. "It wouldn't be hard for me to play them."

"How can he get a badge for that?" whispered Lisa to Molly.

Molly wondered too. But if Mrs. Peters said it was music, it was music. A Scout leader did not lie. If you couldn't trust a Scout leader, who could you trust?

By now everyone was getting tired. Tired of making music. And tired of listening to music. Babies were fussing. Children were yawning. It was time for the last person to play. The last person was Sonny.

"Poor Sonny!" said Molly. "I'd hate to be last. Everyone wants to go home."

"I thought Sonny said he wasn't coming," said Kevin.

"His mom made him," said Kenny.

Mrs. Betz was giving Sonny a little shove. Sonny and the violin. Sonny took the violin out of the big case. He put it under his chin. The Pee Wee Scouts laughed.

"He looks so funny!" whispered Patty.

Sonny lifted his bow and drew it across the violin strings.

It made a loud screeching noise. The Pee Wees covered their ears.

Sonny kept running the bow across the strings. The more he played, the tighter the Pee Wees covered their ears. And the worse the faces they made.

Baby Nick jumped like he was frightened, and then he began to cry. He didn't just cry. He wailed.

When he began to wail, the two dogs threw their heads back and began to howl. They howled and howled and howled. There was so much noise with the howling and wailing that Molly could hardly hear the screeching violin.

The only ones who did not have their ears covered, and were not howling or wailing, were Larry and Mrs. Betz. They were leaning forward listening to every note that Sonny was playing. They had proud smiles on their faces.

Now a baby was screaming so loud, he was turning purple. All of a sudden Sonny burst into tears. He threw his new violin down on the floor and ran out of Mrs. Peters's front door. Mrs. Betz and Larry excused themselves and ran out after him. Mrs. Peters walked to the front and held up her hand again.

"Our little music fest is over, and now we will give out the music badges," she said.

Mrs. Peters was acting like nothing had happened, thought Molly. Sonny had made a fool of himself. Everyone had laughed at

him. Even the dogs! And Mrs. Peters was acting like it was a perfectly ordinary meeting and was going to give out badges!

"Mrs. Peters!" shouted Molly. "We can't give out badges. Sonny isn't here."

Mrs. Peters went to the door and looked out. Mrs. Betz and Larry were trying to reason with Sonny. They tried to get him back into the house. But Sonny would not budge. He sat in a pile of snow and cried.

"It's getting late," said Mrs. Peters to the Scouts. "Sonny can get his badge later."

"Sonny gets a badge for that racket?" yelled Roger. "For hurting our eardrums?"

But Mrs. Peters was calling names. She was pinning badges on the Pee Wee Scouts. And she was doing it fast, because the babies and dogs were still howling.

"I'm sorry our concert had to end like this," she said when all the badges but Sonny's were handed out.

People thanked Mrs. Peters. Then they

trooped out into the dark and started home. They were not as cheerful as they had been when they had come. Several of the men helped Mrs. Betz and Larry pick up Sonny, who was thrashing about, and carry him.

"He's really upset," said Molly.

"Baby," said Rachel. "His mother shouldn't have made him take violin lessons. That's what happens when you are forced to do something."

"He'll get over it," said Roger. "By tomorrow he'll be his old dumb self again."

"I hope so," said Molly, waving good-bye to Mary Beth.

But Roger was wrong.

CHAPTER 6
Sonny Runs Away to Alaska

The next morning Sonny was not his normal self. At nine o'clock Mrs. Betz found a note on his pillow. She called Molly's mother and read it to her over the phone. It said:

I went to Alaska. Don't try to find me.

Mrs. Duff called the other parents. "We have to help find Sonny," she said. "Come over as quickly as you can."

Everyone gathered at Molly's house. From there they went to the Betzes'. Molly had been eating breakfast. She took her toast along with her.

"We put Sonny to bed last night," sobbed Mrs. Betz, "and when I went in this morning to call him for his favorite TV cartoon, he was gone."

Poor Sonny, thought Molly. Rachel had been right. Mrs. Betz should not have made Sonny take violin lessons. Lots of Pee Wees had been upset in the past. But none had ever run off to Alaska.

"I am sure he is somewhere nearby," said Mrs. Peters.

"We'll find him," said Mr. Peters.

The fathers gathered together and went out looking for Sonny.

"Do you think he's really in Alaska?" asked Mary Beth.

"Naw," said Roger. "How could he get there? You need a ticket or something, you can't just walk. It takes a long time to go so far."

"Maybe he went on a dogsled," said Tim.

Molly was worried. Whether he was in Alaska or not, Sonny was hurt. He was embarrassed. He couldn't face the Scouts again. She had her music badge, but it did not make her happy this time. Sonny did not have his, and Sonny was a friend. Even if he was a baby.

"He could freeze in Alaska," said Tracy. "My cousin got frostbite in Minnesota last year."

Tracy was right. Sonny could freeze right in their own town. It was winter. What would he eat? Where would he sleep?

Molly worried more about Sonny than the others did. She knew what it was like to be laughed at. To make mistakes in front of others. Once the elastic in her underwear had broken and her panties fell down. She ran away that time. Away from the Scout meeting. But she had run to her own home.

"I'll bet Sonny is home somewhere hiding

from his mother,'' said Molly. ''Let's go look around his house.''

Several of the Scouts ran to Sonny's house. They looked under bushes and in the garage. They looked in the windows to see if Sonny was behind the couch. They saw his violin, but no Sonny.

Molly pounded on the door. ''Sonny?'' she called. ''Come out. We are your friends.''

The Pee Wees called and called. But no one answered. Sonny was nowhere in sight.

''Maybe he is at the library,'' said Patty.

The Scouts ran to the library. But it was closed. ''It's not open on Sunday!'' said Molly.

''School!'' said Roger. ''He's probably hiding out at school. He thinks we wouldn't look for him there.''

''The school is locked up,'' said Kenny, shaking his head. ''It's Sunday, and it's vacation. They really lock schools up tight during vacation.''

"Sonny likes candy," said Tracy. "He could be downtown at the candy store."

The Scouts raced downtown. The stores were open for Christmas shopping. People were everywhere. They were carrying big bags.

"How can they shop when Sonny is lost?" cried Molly. She felt mad at all of them, smiling and singing and laughing. Christmas was not going to be a happy one if Sonny was in Alaska freezing his feet.

The Scouts went from store to store asking people if they had seen someone who looked like Sonny.

"He's short," said Roger to an old man. "About this tall." Roger held his hand up to his chest. "He's still got training wheels on his bike."

"What difference does that make?" demanded Mary Beth. "He isn't riding his bike in the snow, or in the stores!"

Poor Sonny. How was he ever going to

grow up if everyone only remembered what a baby he was?

The Scouts headed for home, looking in the churches and drugstores along the way.

"What will Mrs. Betz do with Sonny's presents on Christmas?" Lisa asked.

Molly thought of the Betzes' tree with all the boxes under it marked SONNY. All unopened, even on New Year's.

"She can save them for next year," said Tim. "In case he comes back."

"Mrs. Betz will probably take all the presents and go to Alaska," said Kevin. "She'll have to look in all those igloos till she finds Sonny."

"He'll probably have one of those Eskimo suits on," said Tim. "Made out of whale fur."

"Whales don't have fur," scoffed Rachel. "They have blubber."

When the Scouts got to Molly's house, the search party of fathers was just returning. Mr. Duff looked dejected.

"He'll come home on his own when he gets hungry," said Mr. White with a weak laugh. But no one else laughed.

Sonny wouldn't come home when he was hungry. Molly knew that. He was hurt. Really hurt. And food didn't matter when you felt that bad.

"I guess," said Mary Beth's father, "we will have to call the police."

CHAPTER 7

The Police and Molly's Secret

The Pee Wees jumped when they heard the word *police*. When the police were called in, it meant serious business. Sonny really was lost.

The word *police* scared Molly. But at the same time she felt relieved. Police could find anyone. They had dogs that could probably sniff Sonny out even if he was as far as Alaska.

"What a shame," said Molly's mother when everyone left, "such a nice afternoon at the music fest yesterday had to end so badly. Poor Sonny. And Mrs. Betz is going crazy with worry."

"We'll find him," said Mr. Duff. "He might even have come home by himself by now."

But Mrs. Duff called Mrs. Betz, and he hadn't. Molly could hear Mrs. Betz crying on the telephone.

Molly went upstairs to her room to think about what to do. She pinned her new badge on her scarf with her other badges. Then she lay down on her bed to think about where Sonny could be, and fell asleep. She dreamed she was locked in a giant violin case and couldn't get out. Someone picked the case up and put it on the back of a truck. "Let me out!" shouted Molly, pounding on the case. No one heard her. And all she could hear was the sound of people laughing and dogs howling and babies crying. Molly began to cry in her dream. She cried so hard, she woke herself up.

Molly sat up on the side of her bed. She was awake now, so the crying should stop. But it didn't! She could still hear it! Sobbing and sniffing and nose blowing. Molly pinched herself to see if she was awake. She was. Wide awake. Then who was crying? Was it a ghost?

Molly got up and looked out in the hall. No one was there. She looked in her mother's sewing room. No one. She followed the sound of the crying. It seemed to be coming from the bathroom!

Molly went into the bathroom and the sounds grew louder. But she couldn't see anyone. Was it coming out of the wall?

Then Molly gave the shower curtain a pull. And there, in her very own bathtub, was Sonny Betz! And he was crying.

"Sonny!" said Molly. "What are you doing in my bathtub?"

"I'm hiding," he said. "I'm never going home again as long as I live."

"You aren't in Alaska after all," said

Molly. She was glad Sonny was alive and well, but she was disappointed Alaska was just a tall tale. It didn't take much courage to hide in a bathtub.

Sonny wiped his nose. He had his gym bag in the bathtub with him.

"Do you know how much it costs to go to Alaska?" asked Sonny. "A lot more than I've got in my bank. I thought it would be cheaper to hide in your house."

Molly groaned. She was just about to tell Sonny she was going to call his mother, when he said, "You've always been nice to me. Even when the other kids laugh and call me names. You never call me names. You're my best friend."

It was not easy being someone's best friend. Molly did feel sorry for Sonny. But how could she hide him here when the police were out looking for him?

"The police are looking for you," said Molly. "They'll find you anyway."

"Not here," said Sonny. "They won't look in your bathtub."

Molly had to admit they wouldn't look there.

"But my mom and dad take showers," she said. "They'll come up to take a shower and see you."

"I can go in your closet when they take a shower," said Sonny. "I can't go home. Not ever. Don't make me go home!"

Sonny hung on to the towel bar as if Molly might try to carry him away. She couldn't turn him in. Sonny trusted her.

"You can stay till I figure something out," said Molly.

Sonny threw his arms around Molly and clung to her. "Thank you," he sobbed.

"You can't stay here forever," said Molly.

Sonny seemed satisfied. He was unpacking his gym bag. He hung his shirts and shorts on the towel bars. He took his toothbrush out and put it on the bathroom sink. Then he unrolled a little blanket. It looked like a baby blanket. It had little animals and clowns on it. Sonny spread it out in the bathtub.

"This is my bed," he said. "I can sleep right here."

Sonny was moving in! Molly was harboring someone who was hiding from the law. Would the police put her in jail when they found out? She thought of how upset her parents would be. She pictured them coming and visiting her in jail. Handing her books and candy through the bars during visiting hours. Did jails have visiting hours like hospitals? Would she have to wear a striped suit with a number on it?

"Molly," called Mrs. Duff, up the stairs. "Come and eat lunch, dear."

"Bring me something good," said Sonny. "I'm starving to death."

Sonny stretched out to take a nap.

He was definitely settling in. Molly supposed he had to eat. She couldn't starve him.

Even fugitives got hungry. Even jails fed convicts.

"Be quiet," said Molly. "Don't make any noise up there or my dad will be suspicious."

Sonny nodded.

Molly ran down the steps and into the kitchen. She sat down at the table for lunch. Tomato soup! How could she put that in her pocket for Sonny? It would run all over.

Molly's father offered her a grilled cheese sandwich. She took two. When her mother got up to get the salt and her dad was busy eating, she slipped one sandwich into her pocket.

It wouldn't be enough. Sonny was a big eater. When no one was watching, she put a few chips into her pocket and another sandwich in her other pocket.

"Please pass the sandwiches," said Molly politely.

"You seem awfully hungry today," said her dad. "That is your third grilled cheese."

"I feel too worried about Sonny to eat," said Molly's mother.

"I think Sonny is close to home," said Molly. "It's awfully expensive to go to Alaska."

She took a cookie from the plate and slipped it into her pocket on top of the sandwich and chips.

"Imagine how Mrs. Betz feels," said her mother.

"I don't think she should worry," said Molly. "He's around here somewhere. Sonny's not too brave, you know. He's kind of a baby."

She hoped Sonny hadn't heard her say that.

"Do you really think he is nearby?" said Mrs. Duff hopefully.

"I know he is," said Molly with her pockets bulging.

Then she excused herself and washed her hands and ran back upstairs.

Sonny was waiting. He stuck his head

through the shower curtain and said, "Did you get me something good?"

Molly reached into her pockets.

"I don't like cheese," he said when he saw the sandwiches.

Molly put the food on a paper napkin and handed it to Sonny.

"Where's a plate?" he demanded.

"You'll have to eat without one," said Molly. She was losing her patience with Sonny. Did he think she was running a home for runaway children?

"I'm still hungry," Sonny said when he finished the cookie. "Can you get me some more?"

Molly shook her head. "They'll get suspicious," she said.

Just then there was a commotion downstairs. The doorbell rang and the sound of voices was heard.

"Molly?" called a voice. "I'm coming up to see you!"

CHAPTER 8
Good News and Bad News

Sonny dived into the tub. "Hide!" he called.

Molly closed the bathroom door and went out into the hall. Mary Beth was running up the steps.

"Don't come up!" yelled Molly. "You can't—" But Molly didn't know how to finish the sentence. She wondered if she should say she had some contagious disease.

But Mary Beth was her best friend. She couldn't lie to her.

"Why can't I come up?" Mary Beth demanded.

All of a sudden Sonny sneezed.

"Who's up here?" demanded Mary Beth. "Who's in the bathroom?"

Molly sighed. "It's Sonny," she said.

Mary Beth opened her mouth to scream, but Molly ran over and put her hand over it. "Shhhh," she said. "I said I wouldn't tell."

"That's why we're here," said Mary Beth. "Everyone is looking for Sonny. Even the police. You have to tell."

Before they knew it, Rachel came bounding up the steps too.

"Your mom said I could come up," she said. "Everyone is meeting here to talk about Sonny."

"He's here," said Mary Beth, pointing to the bathroom.

All of a sudden the bathroom door opened. "What is this?" said Sonny. "A Pee Wee Scout meeting or something? I thought you said you wouldn't tell," he said, looking at Molly.

"Nobody knows but us," said Rachel, running into the bathroom.

But just then Roger came up the steps. "I came with my mom and dad," he said. Then he stopped and stared at Sonny.

Sonny pushed the others into the bathroom. "You can't tell," he cried. "You can't tell them I'm here. I'm never going back home again. I won't play that violin. Never never never."

Even Roger looked like he understood. "You really sounded dumb," he said. "That thing sounded like a squeaky door."

Sonny burst into tears and Rachel gave Roger a shove.

"I have an idea," said Molly. "What if your mom didn't make you take violin lessons?" she said to Sonny. "Would you go home then?"

"I'm not playing that violin," he said. "I'm not going home."

Molly stamped her foot. It was hard to not lose her temper at Sonny. "If your mother said you never had to play the violin again," she said, "would you go home? Remember, you can't stay here long."

This time Sonny seemed to listen.

"It's getting too cold to live outside," said Mary Beth.

"You won't have any food," said Rachel.

"You won't get any Christmas presents," said Roger.

Molly looked at Sonny's clothes hanging from the towel bars. She looked at his toothbrush on the sink. "My dad will be taking a shower up here tonight," she said.

"I might go home," said Sonny, wiping his eyes, "if I never ever have to play that thing again."

"Good," said Molly. "Now I have to talk to Mrs. Betz."

Sonny stayed in the bathtub and the other Scouts tumbled downstairs. Molly ran up to her mother and said, "I have to talk to you right away."

"We can't talk now, Molly. We are having a meeting about how to find Sonny."

"Go and play while we meet," said Mr. White to Roger.

Molly's dad was holding up a map of the city. He was putting pins on places where they would go look.

"But I have to talk to Mrs. Betz," said Molly. "It is important."

"We don't want to disturb her now," said Mrs. Peters.

All of the Pee Wees who were there shook their heads. But the grown-ups went on planning places to look for Sonny.

Molly went into the kitchen. She picked up the phone and dialed Mrs. Betz's number.

"I am sorry to disturb you," said Molly

politely. "But I have some good news, and some bad news."

Mrs. Betz appeared to be listening.

"Sonny is fine. He is here in my bathtub. He won't come home unless you say he doesn't ever have to play the violin again."

"Is she happy?" whispered Mary Beth.

"Did she say he can quit lessons?" asked Roger.

When Molly hung up, she ran up to Sonny. "Your mom says you never have to take lessons again," she said. "She said she had no idea you hated the violin so much."

"Did she put it in writing?" asked Sonny. "My mom gets stuff in writing. I want it in writing that I don't have to take lessons ever again. I want her to sign it."

Molly stamped her foot. "You can trust your own mother," she said.

"No, I can't," pouted Sonny.

"Come on," said Roger. "We can go over to his house and get her to write it down."

The Pee Wees all crept silently out the back door to the Betz house. Sonny came, too, with his gym bag. "I'll wait outside till she writes it," he said.

When the Pee Wees knocked on the door, Mrs. Betz hugged them. She had tears in her eyes. Larry was calling the police department to tell them Sonny was found.

"He wants it in writing," said Roger. "About the violin."

Now Mrs. Betz began to laugh. She found a piece of paper and wrote down: "Sonny: You do not have to play the violin again. I will give it away. Love, Mom."

When Sonny saw it, he rushed in the back door and up to his room.

"So Sonny was at your house all this time," said Larry.

"In my bathtub," said Molly. "He couldn't afford to go to Alaska."

Mrs. Betz called the Duffs and they told the rest of the Scout families. They all came over for a party to celebrate Sonny's homecoming. Mrs. Peters passed warm drinks and snacks all around. Pretty soon Sonny smelled food and came down.

"I had no idea Sonny was so unhappy with the violin," Mrs. Betz reported. She had her arm around Sonny. She was holding him tight.

"Can I have another glass of soda pop?" asked Kevin.

"Molly, would you get more soda for everyone, from the kitchen?" asked Mrs. Betz.

Kevin went along to help her carry the glasses. He got ice from the freezer.

"Where does Mrs. Betz keep the bottles of pop, I wonder?" asked Molly. She opened one of the cupboard doors. She saw the soda, but she also saw something else.

"Look!" she said, pointing. "Look what is up on the top shelf!"

"The vase!" said Kevin. "Mrs. Peters's antique vase! Mrs. Betz stole it!"

"I don't think she stole it," said Molly. "Sonny's mother wouldn't steal a vase."

"I knew I'd find it! Didn't I tell you I'd find that vase?" shouted Kevin.

Molly looked worried. "We'll have to tell the insurance company," she said. "And they will take away Mrs. Peters's piano."

Now Kevin looked worried too.

Molly got up on a chair and took down the vase. Just as she was stepping to the floor, the kitchen door opened and Mrs. Peters came into the kitchen. Molly was so surprised, the vase slipped out of her hands and onto the floor. It smashed into a million little pieces.

"My vase!" shouted Mrs. Peters. "Now I remember! I loaned it to Mrs. Betz for a party she was having! She must have forgot she had it!"

"It's broken," cried Molly. "And it's all my fault."

Just then Mr. Peters came into the kitchen, along with other parents and Scouts. They all looked at the broken vase.

"Now we don't have to return the money to the insurance company!" said Mrs. Peters. "We don't have to give up the piano! Molly saved the day!"

"But your pretty vase," said Molly.

"It was an accident," said Mrs. Betz.

"And a good one," laughed Roger.

"I never did like that vase anyway," said Mr. Peters. "I like the piano a whole lot better."

Larry swept up the glass and everyone had some more soda pop and snacks before they left.

"This is a Christmas we won't forget," said Molly's mother, putting her arm around her daughter.

"And neither will Sonny and his mother," said Mrs. Peters.

It was evening when all the Scouts and their families walked home through the snow. When Molly got into her bed, her mind was spinning with all that had happened.

She had a new badge.

She had been a friend to Sonny.

She'd solved the mystery of the missing vase.

And she had accidentally helped Mrs. Peters keep her piano.

As if this wasn't enough, there was still Christmas Day coming up, with gifts and dinner and tree lights and friends. That was enough excitement for any Pee Wee Scout!

Molly turned over and fell asleep.

Pee Wee Scout Song

(to the tune of
"Old MacDonald Had a Farm")

Scouts are helpers, Scouts have fun
Pee Wee, Pee Wee Scouts!
We sing and play when work is done,
Pee Wee, Pee Wee Scouts!

With a good deed here,
And an errand there,
Here a hand, there a hand,
Everywhere a good hand.

Scouts are helpers, Scouts have fun,
Pee Wee, Pee Wee Scouts!

☆ Pee Wee Scout Pledge ☆

We love our country
And our home,
Our school and neighbors too.

As Pee Wee Scouts
We pledge our best
In everything we do.

by Juanita Havill
illustrated by Stanford Kay

Scott Foresman

Editorial Offices: Glenview, Illinois • New York, New York
Sales Offices: Reading, Massachusetts • Duluth, Georgia
Glenview, Illinois • Carrollton, Texas • Menlo Park, California

"Amanda is very independent," Mrs. Baxter told me. She was going to the movies with Mr. Baxter and had called me to baby-sit her daughter.

"What time should Amanda go to bed, Mrs. Baxter?" This was my first baby-sitting job, and I wanted to do a wonderful job. Then maybe the Baxters would ask me back and tell their friends that I was a good baby-sitter. I was also hoping Amanda didn't have unlimited playtime hours before bed. I had homework to do!

Mrs. Baxter told me Amanda went to bed at eight, and then she told me what to do for supper. "I've already prepared supper. Just warm it up in the toaster oven. Fifteen minutes at three hundred degrees."

Just then Amanda came into the kitchen. She had big, brown eyes and wavy, blonde hair. She was wearing a pink and white checked skirt and white blouse, and she stared up at me with intense interest.

I wondered if I should smile. She looked so serious. Besides, I have a wide smile with what looks like miles of metal on my teeth. It would probably scare her. My mouth felt paralyzed. *Get a grip on yourself,* I thought, and I smiled a little smile with my mouth closed.

"Hi, Amanda. I'm Grace."

"Are you from China?" she asked.

"No," I said. "I was born right here in San Diego." I was ready for this question. People who don't know that my grandparents came from Vietnam sometimes ask me that.

"Me too," Amanda said. "I was born in San Diego." She took my hand and pulled me toward the counter on the other side of the kitchen. "Do you want to see Scuttle?"

"Good-by, Amanda," her mother said, and Amanda ran to give her a hug. Mr. Baxter hurried into the room and she hugged him too.

As soon as they left, Amanda showed me a cage on the kitchen counter. In it, a little furry creature was running around in an exercise wheel.

"This is Scuttle." Amanda reached in, and a little ginger and white fur ball crawled into her hands. She took him out. "He's the class hamster, and this is my weekend to bring him home."

It made me a little nervous to see Scuttle outside the cage. What if Amanda dropped him? He could get hurt. She was careful though, and Scuttle didn't squirm or panic while she stroked his head. His nose even stopped twitching for an instant.

"Cute!" I said.

Suddenly a silky gray cat jumped onto the counter. Scuttle, who had been sniffing and bobbing his head to look around, froze at the sight of the cat. Paralyzed except for his trembling nose, he stared at the cat.

"Get down, Missy," Amanda scolded the cat.

I scooped my hand under the cat's chest and carried her to the back door. "Can Missy go outside?" I asked. "I think she shouldn't be around while Scuttle's out of his cage."

"It's okay. Missy goes out all the time," said Amanda.

I set Missy outside on the back step. She licked her shoulder a couple of times then strolled off as if to say, "I'm not interested in your little fur ball anyway."

"You don't have any more predators around, do you?" I said. "I mean cats or dogs."

"No, just Missy." Amanda held Scuttle toward me. "You can pet him," she said.

I touched his soft furry head. "Look how tiny his feet are," she said.

"He's cute," I said, "but be careful, Amanda. You wouldn't want him to get loose." I felt a lot better when Amanda put him back in his cage.

I was surprised at how fast the time went by that evening. After supper we went out to the swings in the backyard. Then it got dark and Amanda wanted to play games inside. Missy followed us into the house. She went into the living room and sat right on top of the cards for a game called "Memory."

"I guess Missy wants to play," I said and scooted her off the cards.

"Missy plays with me sometimes," Amanda said, "but it's more fun to play with you, Grace. I have to turn Missy's cards over for her."

Amanda didn't make a fuss when I told her at eight o'clock it was time to get ready for bed. I told her I would read her stories or tell her made-up ones. That made her happy. Actually she did manage to stay up past eight-thirty but only because we talked for a while. I got carried away with a story about a rainforest that I made up on the spot. It was a good story and I thought I could use it for our book project at school. I sat in her room until she fell asleep, and then I tiptoed to the kitchen.

I went to get my homework from my backpack on the counter by the hamster cage. Scuttle saw me and stretched up on his hind legs toward me like a little kid wanting to be picked up. I opened the cage door and stuck my hand in. Scuttle sniffed around my fingers, tickling me with his whiskers. Then he crawled onto my palm, and I lifted him out of the cage.

He was furry and soft, and his eyes sparkled like shiny beads. I stroked his tummy, and then suddenly he leaned over and scratched my finger. In surprise I loosened my grip. Scuttle slipped between my fingers, scuttled along the counter onto a stool, and then onto the kitchen floor. In a wink the speedy hamster dashed into the living room. I ran after him in a panic and caught a glimpse of him running behind the upright piano in the corner.

I crouched down and tried to see behind the piano and then under it, but Scuttle was hidden from sight. I knew I had to catch him somehow, and then the solution popped into my mind. I would make a trap. I had to work fast because I didn't want Scuttle to come out and run behind something else. Hiding places for a hamster were unlimited in this house. I found the top of a gift box in a trash can. Next I needed a clothespin and found one in the laundry room. I tied a long piece of string around it—string from a kitchen drawer—and balanced the box on the clothespin about a foot from the piano.

Scuttle wasn't going to crawl into my box trap without a strong reason, so I got some of his seeds and pellets from the dish in his cage. I dropped them in a line from the piano and made a little pile under the box.

I tried to keep from panicking as I stretched out on the floor holding the string in my hand and watching for signs of Scuttle.

There he was with his wiggling nose and twitching whiskers. He picked up a pellet and popped it in his mouth, and then grabbed a piece of corn. He was getting close to the box.

"Grace, what are you doing?" said a sleepy voice from the doorway.

I jumped up in surprise, and Scuttle scuttled back under the piano.

"Oh, Amanda, you scared me for a minute. It's a long story. I'm trying to trap an animal."

"A wild animal in the house?"

"It's not exactly wild."

"Is it dangerous?" Amanda asked.

"No, not dangerous," I said. "But he can bite, and he is very independent. He doesn't like being in a cage, I guess."

Amanda's mouth dropped open. "Scuttle!" she shouted. She looked around frantically. "Where's Missy?"

Then paralyzed with fear, I watched Missy run like a cheetah across the living room and dive toward the corner of the upright piano. I had a sinking feeling that this was going to be the most memorable experience in my short baby-sitting career . . . but not the kind of memorable evening I had hoped for.

I snapped into action and ran after Missy. I picked her up and took her down the hall to the playroom. Then I set her down and closed the door behind her.

I went back to the living room. "Missy must have terrified Scuttle. He's probably paralyzed with fear and won't move the rest of the night."

"I have to take him back to school tomorrow!" Amanda sounded upset.

I could see tears beginning to well up in her eyes. I noticed it was nine o'clock already. "Don't worry," I said. "We'll coax him out. What does he like to eat, even more than his hamster food?"

"He likes crackers and cereal and—I know—cashews," Amanda said. She ran to the kitchen and got a can of mixed nuts, and we managed to find four cashews.

I set the cashews in a line from the piano to the box, and we sat down and held very still waiting for Scuttle to come out. For ten minutes we sat frozen, barely even breathing. Then Scuttle inched out again. His whiskers twitching, he crawled up to the first cashew and popped the whole nut into his cheek pouch.

Scuttle picked up the next cashew and the next, stuffing them into his mouth. The hamster seemed to have unlimited space in his cheeks for the large nuts. Scuttle hesitated at the fourth one, as if the box made him nervous. Then he dashed toward the fourth cashew, and the instant he was under the box, I jerked the string. The clothespin flew up in the air and the box flopped down over Scuttle.

Amanda and I hurried to the box. I lifted it a little bit, and Amanda reached in and gently coaxed Scuttle until she could hold him in her hands. I opened the cage door and she set Scuttle on a bed of shredded newspapers and wood chips. The look Scuttle gave us was memorable. His cheeks stuck out like lumpy saddlebags and his black eyes beamed.

"We did it. And thanks, Amanda."

"How did he get out?" she asked me.

I told her the truth, even if it made me feel a little silly. "He was so cute. I picked him up and you know what? He scratched me and I let him go."

"He never nips or scratches . . . unless you rub his tummy."

"Oh," I groaned.

We heard car wheels crunching the gravel in the driveway. Amanda ran for her bedroom. I followed her and tucked her back into bed.

"Good night, Amanda," I said. "Sleep tight."

"I hope you come again soon, Grace," Amanda said.

"Me too. This was a memorable evening all right," I said. Then I went down the hall to let Missy out and talk to Amanda's parents.